DANGER ZONE

extreme survival

by ANTHONY MASTERS

Illustrated by Tim Sell

W
FRANKLIN WATTS
LONDON•SYDNEY

EXTREME SURVIVAL

This edition published 2003 by
Franklin Watts
96 Leonard Street
London
EC2A 4XD

Franklin Watts Australia
45-51 Huntley Street
Alexandria
NSW 2015

Series editor: Helen Lanz
Art Director: Robert Walster
Designer: Sally Boothroyd
Special Needs Consultant: Pat Bullen,
Head Teacher of Moderate Learning
Difficulties, Bitham School
Reading Consultant: Frances James

A CIP catalogue record for
this book is available from
the British Library.

ISBN: 0 7496 5052 4

Printed in Great Britain

Contents

DANGER ZONE

FACT FILE

LOCATION

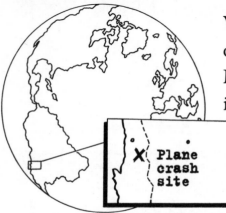

X Plane crash site

Western side of the Andes Mountains in Chile

DANGER

Plane crash in snow-covered mountains with Uruguayan rugby team and friends on board

PERSONNEL

Roberto

Roberto, Nando and other surviving passengers of the Fairchild F-227

Nando

HAZARDS

- ! Bad weather, regular snowfalls
- ! Bitterly cold nights
- ! Search called off
- ! Injuries
- ! Limited food supplies running out fast
- ! No water
- ! Poor clothing

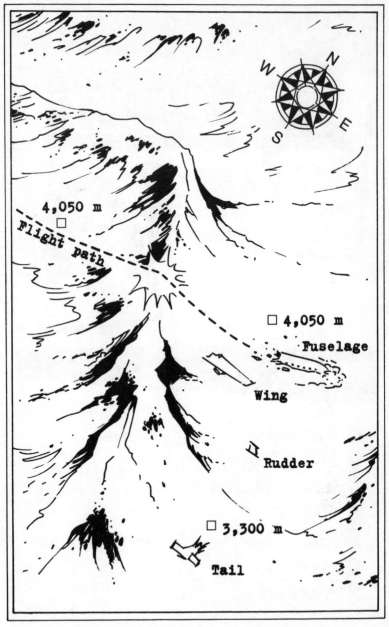

N W E S

4,050 m

Flight path

☐ 4,050 m

Fuselage

Wing

Rudder

☐ 3,300 m

Tail

Map showing crash zone in the Andes

CHAPTER ONE

The Andes Crash

The plane broke through the cloud. The passengers saw the mountainside only metres away from them.

Some prayed. Others held on to the seat in front.

In seconds, the right wing of the Fairchild F-227 hit the side of the mountain and snapped off. The plane spun on to its tail which also broke away.

Some of the passengers were thrown out and killed at once.

The rest of the plane landed the right way up. It slid down a steep valley for hundreds of metres.

Seats broke loose and the bitterly cold air rushed in.

The plane came to a stop. The cabin was filled with the screams of the injured.

Chapter Two

Survivors

The original forty passengers were made up of members of a Uruguayan rugby team, their friends and families. There were also five crew members on board. They were flying from Argentina to Chile.

● A safe way through

The flight was crossing the snow-covered Andes. It was a difficult flight path. The mountains were steep.

There were only two safe ways through the mountain range.

The wind currents made it hard to keep the plane on course.

Bad weather had already delayed the flight. But then the experienced crew had given the all-clear for the journey to continue.

● Badly injured

Now thirteen lay dead. There were thirty-two survivors - many were badly injured.

To their horror, the survivors quickly discovered the radio was broken and the pilot was dead.

● An early rescue?

Gazing up at the mountain peaks they were sure they could never escape on foot. But, at this early stage, they were confident they would be rescued.

It was cold. Snow began to fall at 4 pm.

The jagged hole at the back of the plane let in cold air. Two of the survivors, Roy and Marcelo, built a barrier made of seats and suitcases. The wounded passengers sheltered behind this barrier to keep warm.

That night,
many got drunk
to blot out the cries of the injured.

Chapter Three

Survival Teams

By the morning, three more passengers had died. Twenty-nine remained.

Marcelo checked the supplies left in the wreckage.

Eight bars of chocolate
Five bars of nougat
What is left of the wine
Caramels
Dates
Dried Plums
A packet of salted biscuits
Two tins of mussels
One tin of salted almonds
ore small jar each of
...

Lunch was a square of chocolate and wine in a cap from a deodorant can.

Later that day a plane flew overhead. It
didn't see them.

Miserably, the survivors realised that because
the Fairchild was painted white it blended
with the snow-covered mountains. They
couldn't be seen from above!

They faced another hard night on the
mountainside.

During the night more of the
injured died.

● A good idea

Supplies were running low. The survivors were already very thirsty. It was difficult to melt the snow, and eating the stuff was horribly painful.

Then Fito had a good idea.

Using a rectangle of aluminium foil from the inside of a broken seat, he bent the sides to form a shallow bowl. Then he twisted one corner to make a spout.

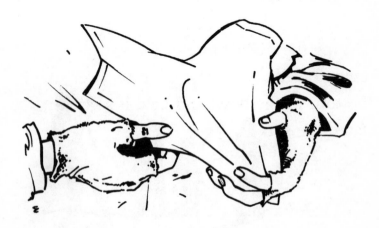

Chapter Four

Escape Attempt

On the fifth day of the crash, a team of four survivors made an escape attempt.

They used seat cushions tied to their feet as snowshoes. But the snow was too deep and the mountains too high.

They were also weak from hunger.

The team turned back, miserably realising how bad the conditions really were.

The feeling of hunger was becoming harder for the survivors to bear. It was the tenth day of being stranded and supplies had almost run out.

Some had tried eating lichen which grew under the snow, but the taste was too bitter.

● The unthinkable

Corpses lay around the plane. The same thoughts passed through the minds of some of the survivors. But these thoughts were unthinkable. It was Roberto who eventually spoke his thoughts out loud.

The others were horrified by what he said. Finally most realised that, however revolting the idea, their only chance of staying alive was to eat the dead.

With a knife, Roberto hacked twenty thin pieces of meat from a frozen corpse. With no fuel to make a fire they couldn't cook the meat - they would have to eat it raw.

● Human meat

Roberto forced a strip of human meat down his throat. Some of the others managed to do the same, hardly able to believe they were eating their dead friends.

That evening, Gustavo wrote a letter to his girlfriend, not knowing if she would ever read it.

'... One thing that will seem incredible to you, it seems unbelievable to me, is that today we started to cut up the dead in order to eat them.'

Chapter Five

No Escape

On a transistor radio found in the wreckage, the survivors heard that the search had been called off.

Before crashing, the plane had got lost in a thick bank of cloud. It had gone off course. The party of survivors was not where the rescue crew expected them to be.

Morale was now very low.

They realised that the only way to live would be to make their own escape.

• Hard going

The next day, three survivors followed the track of the plane up the mountain. They wanted to see what was on the other side.

They were fit rugby players, but they were now weak from lack of food.

The going was hard.

Some more wreckage and corpses were found but, after a freezing night in the open, the group was forced to return. Many mountains lay between them and safety. Escape seemed impossible.

● Another setback

Not long afterwards, the survivors suffered another setback. The batteries of the transistor radio ran out.

This had provided an important link to the outside world.

But worse was to come.

Chapter Six

Avalanche

October 29th, 1972

On the seventeenth day, the plane was hit by an avalanche, killing more survivors.

There were only nineteen left now.

• A tough test

A week later, three survivors, thought to be the toughest, set out to try and escape. Once again they returned, unable to cope with the conditions.

Special efforts would have to be made to prepare a group who *would* manage to get out.

Chapter Seven

Feeling Defeated

A month had passed. One of the nineteen survivors had died and the eighteen people left had still not been found.

On Friday, November 15th, Roberto, Antonio and Nando, now fattened up by cannibalism and prepared for their ordeal, bravely set out towards the north-east.

They were determined to escape and were better equipped.

They took with them a sledge made from half a suitcase. Inside was a bottle of water, more cushion snowshoes, and four rugby socks filled with dried human meat.

● Hard walking

After two hours of hard walking, they discovered the tail of the plane. Inside, they found sugar and three meat pasties which they ate at once.

There were also some woollen socks, batteries, toothpaste and rum.

● Body heat

Now able to make a fire with a lighter they had found in the tail section, the survivors roasted human flesh. After their meal, they each had a spoonful of sugar mixed with toothpaste and rum.

When they tried to move on, the weather was freezing.

That night, they slept miserably on top of each other to share body heat.

● Defeated

The next day was so bitterly cold that Roberto, Antonio and Nando decided to turn back.

They felt utterly defeated.

When they reached the plane, they were told that another survivor had died.

Chapter Eight

An Endless View

The survivors got the radio working again with the new batteries. To their joy, they heard a new search had been mounted.

But Nando, Roberto and Antonio didn't believe any rescuers would find them. For many days, they worked on preparing equipment. This time they had to succeed.

• Despair

On December 11th, another member of the group died. The three men knew they could not delay any longer. The next day they set off. They made good progress.

Nando climbed one of the peaks, but to his despair he discovered only an endless view of snow-covered mountains.

Chapter Nine

A Way Out?

Over to the west were two mountains that were not covered in snow.

Nando, Roberto and Antonio had a discussion. If they climbed down and then walked along the valley to the west, they might get nearer to help.

● Extra rations

They reckoned the journey could take fifty days. They only had enough food for ten.

Nando and Roberto decided to send Antonio back to the plane. With his rations, they could last a little longer.

Their progress was painfully slow, but they knew they had to be careful. One mistake would kill them.

● A valley of flowers

Seven days later, Nando and Roberto arrived in a valley full of flowers and rushing water. They could hardly believe their eyes.

To their joy, they saw a man on the other side of a gorge.

● Afraid

The man threw a note to them, asking how he could help. He seemed afraid.

Nando and Roberto suddenly realised how frightening they must look, with their long hair and beards and dirty clothes.

Nando wrote back:

I come from a plane that fell in the mountains. I am Uruguayan In the plane there are still fourteen injured people.

Later, Nando and Roberto were taken to a village where, at last, they could eat and drink proper food.

It was seventy days since the plane had crashed.

Chapter Ten

Rescued

The fourteen remaining survivors saw the
helicopters flying over the mountains
towards them. The survivors waved
and shouted.

At first, they were horrified as the
helicopters swooped away in the wrong
direction, and seemed unable to see them.

The survivors were desperate. Then, the
helicopter that was in the lead circled above
them. It was shaking in the wind.

At last the rescue operation
had begun!

A stone altar

On January 18th, 1973, members of the
Andean Rescue Corps returned in
helicopters to the site of the crash.

They collected the remains of the dead
and buried them. A stone altar was built
beside them.

A Roman Catholic priest said Mass and the
wreckage was burnt.

The survivors were forgiven for their
cannibalism.

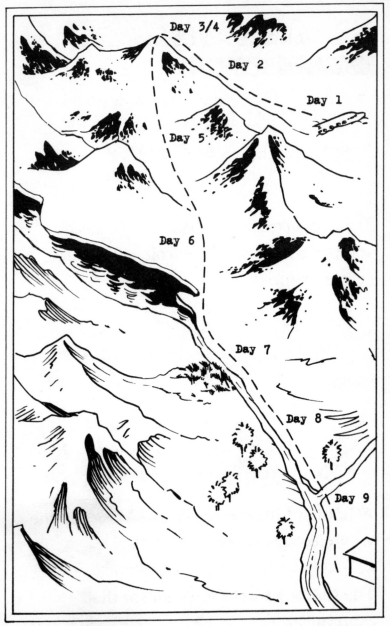

Map showing progress and path to freedom

FURTHER FACTS

- The Andes are the main mountains in South America. They are steep and narrow. The average width across the range is 322 kilometres.

- The Andes rise to an average height of 3,900 metres. Some of the peaks, however, are higher than 6,000 metres. The highest the Fairchild could fly was 6,750 metres. In order to find a safe path, the plane had to fly through a pass in the Andes where the mountains were not as high.

- The snowline lies between 4,200 and 4,800 metres. This is where snow usually falls and remains on the mountains.

- Parts of the Andes above the snowline are always covered in snow. The temperature at night is freezing. There are often snowstorms and avalanches.

- The climate, or weather, in the Andes is very different across the whole range.

- Visibility (the ability to see) is often poor.

- Hot currents of air rise up from the warmer land below the snowline. When the hot air meets the icy air, strong wind currents are formed.

- Cyclonic winds (violent winds that blow in circles) come in from the Pacific Ocean. These winds tear up the valleys from the west and meet the hot and cold currents. As a result, a plane could be blown around. The pilot would stand no chance of staying in control of the plane.

GLOSSARY

Altar: a table used during a religious service.

Avalanche: a mass of snow, containing rock and ice, tumbling down the mountainside.

Cannibalism: when a person eats human flesh or an animal eats others of its own kind.

Corpses: the bodies of dead people.

Expedition: a journey undertaken for a reason. In this case, in order to find a way out of the valley.

Flight path: the official flying route given to every aircraft on every journey to avoid crashes.

Gorge: a steep-sided and narrow valley.

Lichen: a plant that grows on rocks.

Morale: the way a person is feeling - in high or low spirits. It can be affected by a person's mood or situation.

Ordeal: a very difficult experience.

Rations: a fixed amount of food and water.

Snowshoes: special shoes with very large, flat soles that stop a person sinking when walking on snow.

Wind current: a flow of air caused by the wind.

IMPORTANT DATES

1972

October 13th	Fairchild crashes in Andes.
October 14th	More passengers die and survival effort begins.
October 17th	Attempted escape fails.
October 22nd	Cannibalism begins.
October 24th	Second escape attempt fails.
October 29th	Avalanche strikes.
November 5th	Third escape fails.
November 16th	Fourth escape fails.
December 12th	Fifth escape attempt sets out.
December 21st	Survivors reach village.
December 21st	Helicopters begin to lift off remaining survivors from wreckage.

1973

January 18th	Corpses buried and wreckage burnt.